SARAH K. HANS

Dear Krampus

A Monstrous Holiday Romance

For all my monster fucker besties <3

Contents

Foreword

This book is a work of fiction about a woman and her passionate love affair with Krampus and Santa. It's a kinky tale about the healing power of BDSM. As such, there are many explicit sex scenes. The sex is consensual, but Krampus is a sadist who likes to bite, spank, and say humiliating things to our heroine. He also uses his tail in interesting ways.

If any of that sounds like it might trigger you, please step away. Your mental health is more important than this silly book.

For the rest of you, I hope you enjoy this ridiculous tale of spicy Christmas magic. I certainly enjoyed writing it! If you can, please write an honest review on the site of your choice, and tell your friends, or gift them a copy of the book. Reviews and word of mouth are critical for indie authors like me, and I'm so grateful for the support of generous readers like you.

Merry Christmas and Happy New Year,
Sarah

1

The Letter

The cheesy Hallmark movie on my TV reminded me that Christmas was less than a month away and I had nowhere to go. And it was all my own fault.

Over the past year I'd managed to alienate everyone who ever loved me. My parents. My best friend. My boyfriend. Even my boss and my coworkers.

I didn't want to be this person, but there was no escaping my own brain.

I'd tried everything I could think of to get better and failed every time. I'd been hospitalized twice and I'd attended my fair share of support group meetings. I'd taken meds and tried every type of one-on-one counseling. I'd even tried Electroconvulsive Therapy. Nothing worked long-term. The depression always came back like an unwanted ex-boyfriend and with it came irritability, random sobbing fits, and inexplicable rage. Not to mention all the times I just couldn't get out of bed. I couldn't keep a job and I let everyone down, always failing to show up for important events in their lives. I always needed help but never offered it. I was a terrible daughter, sister, employee, and friend.

I took a swig of coconut rum and winced at the sweetness of it as it burned its way down my throat. Booze numbed the pain somewhat, for a while, but not permanently. And the consequences of drinking were always unpleasant—and sometimes, dangerous. I really needed to quit drinking. Again.

Maybe after the holidays.

A plump, jolly Santa Claus walked onscreen and an idea lit up my mind like a string of Christmas bulbs. Santa loved everyone, and he was duty-bound to grant Christmas wishes, right?

I wasn't a child, but maybe he would make an exception this once. My birthday was on Christmas day, after all. Maybe that would grant me special privileges. Even if it didn't work out, what could it hurt to try? Therapists were always trying to get me to write letters—to my inner child, to my parents, to my depression—so maybe it would even be cathartic.

I found a crumpled pad of paper and a ballpoint pen in the junk drawer in my kitchen. I started a letter. My handwriting was shakier than I remembered.

Dear Santa,

I'm writing because I've really messed up my life, and I want to fix it. I've tried everything to get better, but nothing has worked, and things only get worse and worse. Now I'm about to turn 30 and I have no one.

My Christmas wish is to be free of my depression. You're my last hope.

Thank you,

Noelle Jeanette Campbell

I stared at the words and squinted. They wavered on the page. What was I doing? This was ludicrous. What had I done to deserve Santa's kindness? Nothing. All I'd done was hurt people, including myself. I hadn't earned mercy.

What I deserved was punishment.

I balled up the letter and tossed it onto the pile of trash on the coffee table. Then I started another letter.

Dear Krampus,

All I want for Christmas this year is the punishment I deserve for being a terrible person. Please help.

—Noelle

I folded it up, slid it into an envelope, and wrote FOR KRAMPUS on the outside of the envelope. I wondered if anyone had ever written to Krampus before. Should I address it to the North Pole, like I would for Santa? Where did Krampus live, anyway? Did I need to put a stamp on it?

Was sending a letter to an imaginary holiday avatar delusional? Probably. Something new to report to my psychiatrist at our next appointment.

After some internal debate and a lot of rifling through the junk drawer, I found a stamp and stuck it to the envelope just in case. I dropped it in my mailbox and shook my head at myself. At least it would give the mail carrier a good chuckle.

Then I went back to my blanket fort on the sofa to finish watching the movie and forgot about the letter.

2

Christmas Eve

I was rotting on my couch watching heartwarming, romantic Christmas videos when I heard the *clop clop* of something on the roof. I dropped my phone and sat up, staring at the ceiling in surprise.

It was Christmas Eve. Was I about to be robbed? It couldn't possibly be reindeer and a sleigh, right?

The jingle of bells sounded through the ceiling.

That was when I remembered the letter. When I wrote it, I didn't think Krampus could possibly exist. I thought my letter would go nowhere. But now it sounded like Santa was on my roof and the possibility that someone got my letter suddenly seemed very real.

Either that, or I was hallucinating. It wouldn't be the first time.

From overhead, the sounds of footsteps and male voices reached me. Did Krampus bring a friend? A frisson of fear and excitement tickled across my skin. Jumping to my feet, I looked down at the oversize t-shirt I wore with a pair of granny panties and fluffy knee socks. Hardly appropriate attire for meeting a creature out of myth.

A hysterical laugh bubbled out of my mouth. I was probably about to meet a pair of burglars, and I was so delusional I thought one might actually be a mythological goat-man. This was a new low for me.

The fire in the hearth went out abruptly and a pair of black hooves appeared where the flames had been, followed by a massive, dark shape. He reared up in front of the fireplace and I gasped. His brown face was long and clever-looking, surrounded by a tangled mess of dark hair. A pair of horns curved up from his forehead to bump the ceiling. He had a human torso, arms, and hands—covered by a dark leather coat belted at his waist—but below the belt his legs were furry and ended in massive hooves. A sinuous tail lashed behind him that was tipped with a tuft of fur.

His eyes, however, were his most startling feature. They were bright yellow and had the unsettling rectangular pupils of a goat.

Pere Fouettard, aka Father Whipping, aka Krampus, was just as horrifying as I had expected. He was ugly, but he radiated dominance and power like a strong magnetic force.

Krampus was followed by another man who was bearded and wearing red, but otherwise the resemblance to the fat, cheerful, red-suited Santa from Coca-Cola ads stopped there. He wore a fur-lined coat dyed the color of fresh blood that dragged on the floor behind him, and when he pushed back the hood, the face beneath was not the face of a jolly elderly gentleman. Sure, his beard and hair were more salt than pepper, but his cheekbones were high enough to rappel down, his nose was chiseled and slightly crooked, and his eyes were surrounded by long, dark lashes that gave just a touch of softness to his otherwise stony face.

Santa was *hot.*

The fire in the heart blazed back to life once both men were clear of the chimney. Santa and Krampus stared at me, and I stared back, wondering whether I'd finally lost my mind.

"Fuck," Santa said, and it came out a low growl that made me shiver.

Krampus held up a huge hand to stall his partner. "Excuse me, miss," he said to me, his voice deep and full of gravel. He spoke with a thick accent that sounded German or maybe Russian. "Are you Noelle?" His eyes, which were such a bright yellow I could see them even in the dim firelight, roamed my body. A long, pointed, black tongue snaked from his mouth to lick his lips.

Santa dropped his bag and started digging around in his pockets. "We'll have to make her forget."

I took a deep breath to calm my thundering heart and then addressed the monstrous creature before me. "Yes, I'm Noelle. I guess you got my letter." I fidgeted with the hem of my long shirt and hoped they couldn't see the state of my house in the dim firelight. It was a mess, trash everywhere. I did put up a little Christmas tree beside the hearth, but beside these two behemoths it looked embarrassingly tiny.

Krampus's head tilted to the side, his eyes flashing. "And you truly wish to be punished?"

I nodded and swallowed hard. He sounded intrigued. What in the hell was I doing? Fear made goosebumps rise on my exposed skin. Or maybe it was desire. Kind of hard to tell when a supernatural monster was staring me down and licking his lips like that.

"That's not how it works, Mädchen," Santa said, pulling a small pouch from his coat pocket. He started to open it, but Krampus reached over and stopped his hand.

His long face turned slowly back to me. "Tell me why."

I stood on shaky legs and mustered all my courage. "I'm selfish and angry. I lash out at people I love, or I hide from them. I expect too much of them and I hold grudges over minor issues. I'm a burden and I have no one because I can't control my anger. I've tried everything to get rid of it, but nothing has worked. So I think I need to be punished. I think it'll help."

Krampus released Santa's hand to take one step forward. He loomed over me. He was at least 6'5" if you didn't count the horns, and I had to tip my head back to look up at him. "You want to be absolved."

I nodded stiffly and swallowed hard. "Please."

"You're not a child," Santa pointed out.

"But why me?" Krampus asked, ignoring Santa. "Surely there are other humans who would be pleased to help you atone."

"This isn't a big town. Everyone would find out, and so would my family, and I've already humiliated them enough. Besides, you do this, like, professionally, don't you?"

Krampus raised his hand so he could run one finger along the collar of my t-shirt. His skin was incredibly warm and I was surrounded by the scent of cinnamon and nutmeg and something else—something earthy, spicy, and oddly comforting. His yellow eyes flicked to my face. "What's in it for me?"

I took a deep breath, curling my fingers in the hem of my shirt, and then whipped it off over my head, letting it flutter to the sofa behind me. I licked my lips. "Me. I know I'm not exactly a great beauty or anything, but I'll do whatever you want." The idea made a thrill of anticipation race up my spine to harden my nipples.

Krampus chuckled and the sound was like a diesel engine struggling to turn over, low and scratchy. His claw traced a path along the top of one breast, making me shiver. "What a generous offer. Alas, Mädchen, I punish only naughty children."

My bosom heaved with my anxious breaths and....*need*. Desire seemed to bloom where he touched me and spread to the rest of my body, a feeling that reminded me of being drunk. "I've been very naughty. Surely you can make an exception this once?"

Santa chortled. "We don't have time for this." He fidgeted with the pouch.

Krampus's hand shot out at lightning speed and snatched the pouch from Santa's fingers. "We can make her forget later, alter Freund. Let's have a little fun first."

"You know we can't."

"And why not?" Krampus tied the pouch's drawstring to his belt.

That motion drew my eyes down to the massive whip coiled at his side. It was much bigger than I had been expecting. Yikes. I wasn't sure I could survive being struck with that. I started to rethink my whole plan.

"In the sleigh you were just complaining about how you're bored and you never get to do anything but make toys, deliver toys, and argue with me," Krampus said to his companion, though his bright eyes stayed fixed on me. More specifically, on my bare breasts and my peaked nipples.

Santa turned to me. "You weren't naughty this year, Noelle."

"I was. I'm so mean. I push everyone away. I hurt them."

"You have a medical condition. A whipping won't make your depression go away."

I glared at him. "Nothing else has worked."

He frowned and opened his mouth to make another comment.

Krampus barked something at Santa in another language I didn't understand, something thick and angry-sounding. Santa snapped something back in response and crossed his arms over his chest, fixing his companion with a displeased stare.

"Look," I said, interrupting their standoff. "I know it might not be a long-term solution. But let me have one night to feel absolved of all the pain I've caused to myself and others. Just one night." Tears rose in my eyes and I dashed them away.

Krampus's mouth quirked up on one side in a wicked half-smile that revealed a sharp white fang. "C'mon, Nicholas. Look how pretty she is, and how desperate. Can't you feel how this is her deepest wish? Her *Christmas* wish. You wouldn't deny her that, would you?" He flicked his long tongue at me.

Santa said something low and serious in the language they shared. When Krampus nodded, Santa sighed and tossed himself into the overstuffed chair nearby, one leg flung over an armrest. "Fine. But make it quick. We have a lot of presents still to deliver."

3

Punishment

Krampus seated himself on the sofa. It was a plush, over-stuffed affair, made to fit the large living room, but Krampus's enormous body made it look tiny, like one of those sofas for cats. I turned to face him and waited for him to make himself comfortable. I silently hoped he would take control of this situation and tell me what he wanted me to do because I had no idea what I was doing.

I'd never asked anyone to punish me with a whip before. I'd never even engaged in impact play aside from a little light spanking by a reluctant ex-boyfriend. I wasn't a virgin or anything, I'd just never been with anyone very...adventurous.

And here I was offering myself up to a man who appeared to be half goat. Talk about adventurous.

"Dance for us, Mädchen," Krampus said.

I breathed a sigh of relief that he was taking command, something tight in my chest releasing. "Alexa," I called, "Put on sexy music."

The sound of a woman's voice singing sultry jazz filled the house. Krampus smiled, those unnerving yellow eyes watching my every move, unblinking. It was intense.

I swayed and let my body find the rhythm of the music. Eventually my eyes fell shut while I gyrated and undulated to the rise and fall of the woman's voice. With my eyes closed, I could almost imagine I was alone, spending Christmas Eve dancing in my panties and socks. But I could also feel Krampus's eyes on me—and Santa's, too, like twin tractor beams keeping me from drifting off into space.

Eventually, a pair of big, warm hands settled on my hips. I opened my eyes to find Krampus licking his lips again. He'd removed his coat and tossed it on the sofa cushions beside him. My pulse pounded. I let him pull me into his lap, straddling his huge, furry thighs.

"How do you feel, Mädchen?"

"Fine."

"If you wish to stop at any time, say so. Do you understand?"

"If I want to stop, say stop," I repeated back to him. My voice was a quavering whisper.

"Louder than that."

I cleared my throat. "If I want to stop, I'll say stop."

He nodded, looking satisfied.

Krampus's hands went to my ass and pulled me in closer until I rested with my hot center against the thick, hard rod nestled between his furry legs. Like the rest of him, his dick was unbelievably enormous. He bent his head and swirled his long, black tongue around my left nipple, and then my right, his eyes closed as if my skin was delectable. It was the most erotic sight I'd ever seen and I had to close my eyes against the intensity of it, but that only made me more aware of the places his firm, wet tongue explored and the iron ridge on which I rested.

He sucked one of my nipples into his fanged mouth and I

moaned, rocking against his erection involuntarily.

"Yessss," he purred. "Chase your pleasure, Mädchen." And then he affixed his mouth to my nipple again. His big hands pushed my hips down so his rock-hard shaft pressed against my clit.

I rocked harder against him, swept away on a wave of desire that took with it any shame I might have felt about grinding myself to orgasm on a man's lap. No one had ever spoken to me like this before. I was so turned on I couldn't help rubbing against him while he sucked my tits, each in turn, his hands kneading my ass cheeks and keeping me firmly against his hard length. It felt so good, the pleasure winding tighter inside me until I started whimpering and bucking my hips.

Krampus pulled away and turned to Santa, whose presence I had nearly forgotten. "Join us, Nicholas. Look how beautiful she is. And she's so wet. Come feel if you don't believe me." He reached down and slid one clawed finger between us, gliding it over my clit to collect the moisture there, and then holding it up like a trophy. I squeaked with surprise and shivered with pleasure.

Santa snorted. "Hurry up."

Krampus growled. "As if you can't control time."

"It's one night for them, and an eternity for me."

"Then you should join us. It'll pass the time quicker."

Santa snorted at that and looked away.

Krampus returned to laving my breasts with his impressive tongue. I ground against him, clenching my jaw with the effort to find my orgasm. Sweat beaded on my brow and my whole body began to tremble. I was so close, ready to tip over the edge, when Krampus bit down on my nipple, hard, the sharp spike of pain ruining my concentration.

I grunted in frustrated and the Christmas devil laughed, gripping my ass cheeks hard. "Naughty girls don't get to come, Mädchen."

Krampus ordered me to stand. Reluctantly, I slid from his lap and stood before him. I fidgeted with my panties, the gusset of which had disappeared between my labia, now firmly wedged against my clit. Krampus reached out with those sharp claws and shredded the underwear, yanking the remnants of it from my body and tossing them to the floor.

"Turn around," he commanded. When I obeyed, he issued another order: "Put your hands on the mantel. Bend over. "

I bit my lip as shame rushed up over me. No one had ever seen me like this—naked, wanton, flushed and dripping with arousal. I took a deep breath and stepped to the fireplace. I put my hands on the mantel and leaned forward, spreading my legs a little so I could maintain my balance. The fire warmed my face and breasts, but my ass and pussy felt cold, exposed, and vulnerable.

"Look at that, alter Freund," Krampus crooned, rising from the couch. I felt a looming presence behind me just before a warm, callused hand pressed down on my spine, forcing me to arch my back and give both men a better view. "How long has it been since you saw such a beautiful cunt? Come get a closer look."

"Hurry up and get this over with," Santa replied, his voice gruff and tight.

Krampus's hand moved, gently rubbing my left ass cheek. "Now," Krampus said, "It's time for you to take your punishment."

My mouth went dry. "The whip?" The question came out a nervous croak.

Krampus's laugh was low and sensual. "And mark up this

pretty ass? I don't think so." And with that, he swept his hand back and slapped my ass so hard it made a *crack* sound that seemed to split the air.

I gasped and tears sprang to my eyes. It *hurt,* but my pussy clenched hard and a gush of warm wetness between my legs proved I didn't exactly hate it. I clung to the mantel as if it would anchor me to reality.

Krampus wound up again and this time assaulted the other ass cheek. I let out a whimper and a few tears escaped my eyes. He wasn't holding back, not at all. It was incredibly painful, though I wondered how much worse the whip would be.

Probably a lot worse.

I grit my teeth and gripped the mantel harder. I could tell him to stop, or I could walk away, but I wouldn't. I had asked for this, after all. This was my atonement, and I'd bear it, if only so I could forgive myself.

4

The Whip

Crack. Krampus's hand came down for the fifth time—or was it sixth? I'd already lost count in the haze of pain—and a sob escaped me. Behind me, Krampus issued what sounded like a satisfied grunt. His hot breath skated over the irritated, hypersensitive flesh of my rump and his furry tail coiled possessively around my left ankle.

"You're taking your punishment so well, Mädchen," Krampus said, soothing the marks on my ass with one big hand. Then his fingers curled and his claws pricked my skin. His other hand ghosted over my pussy, making me whimper and squirm as conflicting desires warred inside me. I wanted to escape the pain, but I also wanted the spanking, the heavy slap of Krampus's huge hand against my jiggling flesh, accompanied by the praises that drawled from his filthy mouth.

The next smack was to my naked pussy. I cried out, clutching at the mantel, legs shaking. My head dropped, my long hair spilling over my shoulders. When would this end? I prayed it would be soon, or, maybe...never. The pain was delicious, filling me with a sense of peace, and every time he struck me desire flooded my veins like drops of clean, clear water in a pool of filthy pond sludge.

One of Krampus's big hands moved around my waist as if to hold me in place, and something prodded at my pussy lips, something big and hard but cold. "My whip deserves a little fun, too, don't you think?" he purred. The handle of the whip slid between my wet folds and pressed at my entrance. I gasped as he pushed it inside me, the sensation both familiar and strange. It was the same size and shape as a dick or a dildo, but it was cold leather instead of warm flesh or silicone. I imagined the absolutely debaucherous show Santa was getting, watching Krampus slowly insert his whip handle into my dripping cunt while my bare breasts swayed in the open air. I whimpered and shamelessly bucked my hips to help Krampus find the right angle so I could take it all.

Krampus laughed. "Good girl. What a greedy little cunt. If you take my whip so well, you might be able to take my cock." When I jerked in response to his words, he asked, "Would you like that, little Christmas slut? To take my cock?"

I pressed my lips together but nodded. The handle was well inside me now, filling me up, and Krampus stepped back to admire his handiwork. "Nicholas, you must admit, that's a sight to behold: a woman with a whip dangling from her cunt like a tail." His own tail lashed against the carpet with a *thump*.

"Very impressive," Santa replied through what sounded like a clenched jaw.

Krampus slapped my ass again and it pushed the whip handle inside me just a little more. I shouted, writhing, overcome by pain and pleasure, longing to be released from my punishment but also desperate for more, more, *more*. My body shivered so hard my teeth clacked and I moaned in the aftermath of the slap, thrusting my ass higher in the air, my back bowed toward the floor, legs wobbly like a newborn calf's.

Krampus grabbed the whip handle and slid it out of me and back in, slowly at first, then faster. His other hand came around and pressed one knuckle against my clit. I gasped and keened. It felt so good, so amazing, like nothing I'd ever felt before.

Another blow to my pussy shoved the whip handle deep inside me and I screamed.

Krampus laughed as if my pain was uproariously funny, but then someone else was there, someone big, and he was shoving Krampus out of the way. "Stop. Can't you see she's had enough?" The whip handle was abruptly yanked from my pussy and I was bundled into strong arms. My senses were overwhelmed by the scent of peppermint candy canes and warm sugar cookies.

"Santa," I sighed, throwing my arms around his neck.

"Call me Nicholas," he said as he carried my out of the living room and away from the laughing goat-man by the hearth.

"Make sure you taste her tits," Krampus called after us. "They're divine!" Then he lifted the whip handle to his mouth and licked it with his long, black tongue.

5

Comfort

Santa—*Nicholas*—carried me to the master bedroom and into the master bathroom. He kicked the door shut behind him and placed me gently on the floor beside the bathtub. Then he turned the knobs to start water flowing.

While he fussed with the bath, I watched him. He'd removed his scarlet coat and now wore only a linen shirt, wool pants, and a leather belt and boots. In the searing white light of the bathroom I could see his bright blue eyes surrounded by the crinkle of laugh lines. Down his cheek, though, was a long-healed scar. A bit of one ear was missing. He wore his white hair in a messy bun at the back of his head, and I could make out another scar along the side of his skull trying to hide under his hair.

Peeking out from under his shirt were the whorls of a faded tattoo, something that looked traditionally Norse. He rolled up his left sleeve to check the temperature of the water and revealed more tattoos coiling around that arm, faded almost to invisibility, but still there, clinging stubbornly to his immortal skin, telling a story I suddenly needed to know.

Without a word, Nicholas pulled another pouch from his belt and sprinkled something aromatic into the water. Then he lifted me again and lowered my into the warm bath, pulling off my socks as he did. When I hissed at the sensation of water on my burning ass cheeks and sore pussy, he frowned. "It will sting for a moment, but it's good for the wounds."

He was right, and the pain gradually faded. The water wasn't too hot or too cold, as if he'd found the perfect temperature to soothe my irritated skin. "Thank you, Nicholas," I sighed. I sank down into the bath water to my chin and forced myself to relax. If I couldn't relax around Santa Claus, was there any man trustworthy enough for me to let my guard down?

Nicholas shook his head and his blue eyes darkened. "You should not have let him go so far."

"Would he have stopped, if I'd asked?"

His frown deepened. "I don't know. But I could have stopped him sooner."

"It's alright," I assured him, placing one of my hands on the well-muscled forearm that leaned on the side of the tub. I loved a man's forearms, especially when they looked strong. Add tattoos and, well, I was a goner. "I didn't hate it."

"He was hurting you." Nicholas covered my hand with his.

"He was hurting me," I admitted, "but I kind of liked it. And I did ask to be punished. He was just giving me what I asked for."

Nicholas huffed a sigh and heaved himself to a standing position.

I grabbed his hand and clung to it. Water sloshed out of the bathtub at the sudden movement. "Don't leave me, please?"

Nicholas looked unsure, his eyes flicking to the door. "I have a lot of deliveries still to make tonight."

"Is what he said true? That you can control time?"

"Kind of. I can't make the night last forever, but I can make it last however long I need to deliver all the toys. You mortals keep breeding; every year there are millions more deliveries. Even if it's only one night to you, to me it's weeks of hard work to get to everyone. When I started this, I delivered only to a few hundred families." He shook his head and stared at the toes of his boots.

"That sounds like a lot of work you weren't expecting," I said. "That must be frustrating." I didn't mention this was what happened at most jobs—the better your work was, the more efficient you were at doing it, the more work was piled onto your shoulders. I doubted he'd find this comparison helpful. "Could you recruit more elves?"

"There are no elves. That's a common misconception."

"Okay. Could you get help from someone else?"

He looked at me with one silver eyebrow raised. "Who would help? The Easter Bunny?"

That startled a laugh from me. "I don't know. I can think of lots of mall Santas who would be willing to lend a hand, though. And their elves, too."

"And what would I pay them with, reindeer shit?"

I laughed again. "Aren't you being paid with the joy of little children? Why can't your helpers be paid the same?"

"It's not the same for mortals."

"Weren't you mortal once?"

Nicholas glared at me. "Mostly."

"Then can't regular people be made immortal?"

"Odin made me immortal to do this job. I haven't heard from him in centuries. Not sure he's even still around."

"Hmm well, that is a dilemma. Let me think on it." I leaned back in the tub again. My body felt weightless and my eyes, heavy.

Nicholas walked toward the door.

"Don't go," I said.

He hesitated with his hand on the doorknob, his whole body stiff like a statue of a buff Viking warrior.

"Please," I whispered. "I don't want to be alone."

His shoulders sagged and he turned around, but he didn't return to the tub. He leaned against the door with his arms folded over his chest. "I can stay for a little while. Do you feel better, now that you've had your punishment?"

I hesitated to answer. "No. It was a good start, but it wasn't enough."

"I tried to warn you."

I gave a rueful laugh. "You did. But the night's not over."

Nicholas sniffed. "Krampus can punish you with his whip, but you're the only one who can forgive yourself and make things right."

"I know. I do, really. I just feel so worthless. Like everyone would be better off without me. And I wanted to show them all how sorry I was, and maybe if they saw the whip marks on my back they would know, and they'd forgive me."

"Your loved ones don't want your pain, Noelle. They want your happiness."

"Maybe I thought I'd see the whip marks and forgive myself."

Nicholas sank to the floor beside the tub with a sigh. "You should be kinder to yourself. This punishment serves no one. You aren't a bad person, you only made some bad choices. Kindness is the way to improve any situation, not suffering."

I didn't know what to say. "Who is kind to you?"

His eyes widened and then his brows furrowed in thought. "What do you mean?"

"Who is kind to you? Krampus certainly isn't. Is there a Mrs.

Claus?"

He chortled and a pink blush colored his cheeks above his beard. "There's no Mrs. Claus. It's not like in the movies."

"No elves, and no wife. So it's just you and Krampus?"

"And the reindeer."

I sat up in the bath, water sloughing from my shoulders and down the tops of my exposed breasts. Nicholas looked away, his cheeks flushing. "Aren't you lonely? He isn't exactly the nicest companion. Who is taking care of you?"

"No one, if I'm honest."

"Maybe you're the one who needs someone to draw you a bath with magical herbs."

He chuckled. His smile was sad and beautiful and lit up his handsome face. "Maybe. I fear I would neglect a wife. "

My heart thumped hard. "What about a lover? Just someone to have fun with, someone to help you relax once in a while."

He shook his head. "Then the toys might not get made. So many children are counting on me." He sounded resentful, but like he was trying to hide it.

I leaned forward and placed my hand on his arm, gently tracing the whorls of his faded tattoos. "Maybe the children should be counting on their parents more and you, less. You're immortal and you can slow time on Christmas Eve but you're just one man, not a god. At this point I think you've earned a little vacation."

Nicholas held completely still like a spooked deer, but his chest heaved with quick breaths. "That does...sound appealing."

"How long has it been?"

His eyes met mine, clear blue and sparkling like a cenote. "A long, long time."

I let myself move closer to him until my breasts were smashed against the side of the tub and my mouth was only centimeters from his. "Maybe we both could use a little joy."

To my delight, Nicholas closed his eyes and leaned in. When our lips met, electricity sliced through me. I closed my eyes to revel in it. He tasted like peppermint tea and gingerbread. His lips were warm and so very soft. He followed my lead, opening his mouth when I coaxed his lips with my tongue, and then sliding his tongue against mine in a way that made my toes curl.

I was making out with Santa Claus. I was naked, in a bath, with Santa Claus kissing me. A giggle escaped me, interrupting the kiss.

"Sorry, did I...?" Nicholas pulled back and looked at me in horror.

"No, no," I assured him, still grinning. "It's not like that. I was just thinking about how I'm kissing...well, *you*." I traced the shape of his jaw with my fingers. "I didn't expect you to be so hot."

Nicholas chuffed a relieved laugh. "Nobody does. But I wasn't always a toy maker, you know." He leaned back and tugged off his shirt in one quick motion, revealing a muscular torso covered in tattoos and dusted with curly white hair. His stomach was flat but soft, and I liked that. Hot Santa should have a dad bod.

He slapped his belly. "I've had a few too many cookies over the years, I'm afraid."

I sat up, my torso leaving the bath, water sloughing off my breasts. My nipples formed hard peaks in the cold air. "I think you're perfect."

"Are you sure you're up for...recreational activities?" he asked. He studied my face closely. "Krampus didn't take it easy on you."

"I'm sure that if you don't touch me I might die," I confessed. It was only a slight exaggeration. My skin tingled with need like it would burst into flames at any moment unless I felt him against me, naked flesh to naked flesh.

He nodded. "Please excuse my fumbling," he murmured, rising to his knees so he could stare down at me. He took in my face, my breasts, the crux of my thighs, and issued a nervous exhale.

I should have felt self-conscious under his blue stare, but instead I felt warm all over. Nicholas leaned down and kissed me again. One of his arms circled my back, pulling me against him so my breasts were crushed against his bare chest. The other hand explored, trailing fingertips across my wet skin in a way that made me pant and shiver.

Slowly, he lowered me back into the bath. He kept kissing me, exploring my mouth, nipping at my bottom lip and curling his tongue against mine, while his hands roamed. He cupped my breasts and brought one nipple out of the water so he could kiss and suckle it. I moaned, delighted, my hands roving his face, hair, neck and shoulders.

One of his hands slid down my stomach, between my legs. He watched my face as two of his thick fingers slid between my pussy lips, parting them, gliding across my clit and down, down, to my entrance, and then inside, filling me in the most wonderful way. I gasped and arched my back. He smiled, looking pleased with himself. When my tits cleared the water he slid his free arm behind my back to hold me up and attacked my nipples eagerly. His soft beard tickled my skin. The scent of peppermints filled the bathroom.

Nicholas sucked my tits and kissed me and pumped his fingers in and out of me until I was writhing and whimpering in his arms. Finally, he stared my right in the eyes, lowered his thumb to my clit, and said softly, "Now, Noelle, come for me," and I exploded, thrashing and kicking bathwater over the edge of the tub. My vision filled with flashing, flickering lights while bliss coursed through me. I twitched and groaned for several seconds, enjoying one of the longest, most intense orgasms of my life.

When I was limp in his arms, he kissed me over and over again as if I'd died and he would bring me back to life. "That was splendid, Mädchen, splendid." I didn't think I'd done much, but the praise made me light-headed with happiness anyway.

Once I could stand, he lifted me from the tub and dried my dripping body with a towel. He was so careful and thorough I felt like a work of art being prepared for display. I was only a little embarrassed by how old and tattered the towel was, but I didn't get much chance to think about it.

Nicholas dried my feet and looked up at me, smiling. Then he knelt before me and I realized his face was level with my pussy. He leaned forward, slowly, his eyes fixed on my face, and when I didn't protest, he used his fingers to open me to his appreciative gaze. Then his mouth opened, his tongue emerged, and he licked a long, luxurious path up my center.

My legs quivered. "I don't know if I can stay upright if you do that."

He chuckled against my skin. "Then don't stay upright. I can hold you."

I had no doubt he could as I glided my hands across his muscular back and shoulders. He bent his head and licked again. Then his lips closed around my clit and softly sucked, sending tingles shooting from my pussy through the rest of me. I groaned with pleasure and my toes curled against the bathmat.

Without warning, the bathroom door crashed open and a monster appeared in the doorway, making us both jump. Krampus leaned against the frame, whip in hand, grinning so his fangs were prominently on display. His yellow eyes flashed like gold coins. "Well, well, well. Aren't you having a good time. Too bad for you, your punishment isn't over."

Before either of us could react, he stepped forward and threw me over his shoulder.

6

Tinsel

Krampus carried me into the bedroom and tossed me onto the bed. "Look what I have," he growled, showing me the long strands of glittering tinsel he'd tied to the headboard and foot-board. They were silver, like the tinsel on my little Christmas tree. A lump of trepidation formed in my throat and I swallowed it down. I had a feeling Krampus might go too far if I was tied up and unable to stop him, but then Nicholas emerged from the bathroom, tousled and glowering, and I knew he would protect me. Nothing bad would happen to me as long as he was here.

I didn't fight or protest as Krampus tied me spread-eagle to the bed. He giggled like a maniac the whole time. "Look at what a willing little doll she is, our Christmas slut," he said to Nicholas, gesturing to my splayed body. "I can't wait to fill you with my cum, Mädchen."

A shiver ran through me and he laughed, a full-throated chuckle this time. "Have you tasted her, alter Freund?" He grinned at Nicholas, who spluttered. "Ah, you have. Well, my turn, then."

Krampus climbed onto the bed between my legs and lowered

himself to the mattress. He used his clawed fingers to spread my pussy lips and his hot breath gusted across my wet, sensitive skin. I should have been self-conscious, but the rushing of desire drowned out every other thought. "Beautiful," he sighed. He gently swept his knuckle across my clit and I twitched helplessly. That made him chuckle again, and though I couldn't see his face, I could imagine his toothy smile. "Perfect."

And then he lowered his head and devoured me.

Whereas Nicholas had been careful and thoughtful, taking his time and savoring me, Krampus was like a ravening beast. He nipped at me with his sharp teeth, teased me with clawed fingers, and lashed me with his long tongue. He was everywhere at once, fucking me with his knuckles, licking my clit, digging claws into my ass as he held me against his mouth, and then prodding my g-spot with his enormous tongue, pinching my clit, and scraping his claws along the inside of my thigh. It was an overwhelming barrage of sensations that had me writhing and thrusting my hips against his face in moments.

Nicholas appeared at the head of the bed and knelt so he could watch while his companion went to town on my pussy. When I turned to look at him, Nicholas smiled and used one big, callused hand to push sweaty hair back from my face. "Tell me if you want him to stop, Mädchen."

I shook my head. Krampus hummed happily as he continued his work. My pleasure rose higher and higher until I felt like a balloon about to burst, but every time I neared the explosion, Krampus would pull back or change what he was doing to keep me on the edge of bliss. My feet started to hurt from pointing my toes for so long and I thrashed against the restraints that were starting to cut into my wrists and ankles.

"What do you want, Noelle?" Nicholas asked, stroking my

face with one hand and gazing at me with a soft expression on his rugged face.

"I need...you..." I gasped.

"You need me to...suck your tits? Fuck your mouth?"

The words coming out of Santa's mouth were so obscene I almost came on the spot. "T-tell me t-to c-come," I stammered.

Krampus paused in his tongue lashing to shout, "Don't you dare!"

Nicholas smiled, mischief flashing in his blue, blue eyes. "Do you want to come, Noelle?"

"Yes, please, please," I begged.

"How do you want to come?" Nicholas asked.

"On your cock," I confessed, surprising even myself with my bluntness.

Krampus grunted and pulled away from me. "You want Santa to fuck you?"

"Yes, please, more than anything."

Krampus grinned at his companion and gestured to my waiting pussy. "Well, you heard the woman."

Nicholas nodded and rose, stepping around the bed until he was between my legs. He stared at my glistening sex as if hypnotized. I appreciated that he didn't ask me if I was sure I wanted this—surely he was looking at the evidence of my desire right there between my thighs. He untied his wool trousers and pushed them down his hips until he could pull out his cock and pump it with one hand.

Holy fuck. His dick was huge. I shouldn't have been surprised—he was a big guy and it was proportionate to his size—but even so, I found it obscene that Santa even had a cock, much less one so big and hard. The shaft of it was beige like the rest of him, but the mushroom-shaped head was pink and glossy with precum. The balls hanging below were perfectly round and symmetrical. If it was possible for a dick to be beautiful, his was. It could win first place in a dick pageant.

He crawled up the bed, lowering himself on top of me. He slid his hard, hot erection across my pussy lips and swollen clit, making me groan with desperation. I wanted to cant my hips up to bring him inside me, but I couldn't because of the restraints.

"Don't keep her waiting," Krampus barked. To my surprise, he walked up behind Nicholas and grabbed his cock, lining it up with my entrance. Then he pushed down on his friend's ass, forcing him to breach me. Nicholas and I both moaned and Krampus laughed triumphantly, slapping Nicholas's butt cheeks. "There we go. Now get on with it."

Nicholas stared into my eyes as he pushed himself inside me and then withdrew. His eyes rolled back and his eyelids fluttered when he pressed back in, as if my pussy were driving him over the edge. His cock was so big I could swear he would tap my heart if he thrust too hard, so I was grateful he moved slowly, but I also hated him for it, because the long, deliberate strokes were a particular kind of torture. I was so full of him, and then so empty, so full, and then so empty. My entire body sang with need, my awareness narrowed to the place where his cock slid into me and out again.

Krampus slapped his ass a second time. "C'mon, she's already on the edge. Don't torture the poor little slut. Let her come."

"Shut up," Nicholas ordered him, tensing on top of me. He looked down at me again, and maybe he saw the desperation in my face, because he sped up just a little. Soon our hips were slapping together and the quiet of the bedroom was replaced by the wet squelch of his cock hammering away at me.

Krampus leaned down so I could see him looming behind

Nicholas. Nicholas was panting, I was panting, and Krampus was panting, too. I turned my head and saw that the devil had taken his own long, hard shaft in hand and was pumping it furiously. It was huge and dark purple, with a tapered head and a pair of large, furry balls dangling beneath. His black tongue eased from his mouth and licked at his fangs. "Good job, Nicholas. Look at how her tits bounce. I wanna come all over those glorious fucking tits."

"Fuck off," Nicholas snarled, but he did look down, watching my breasts bounce with each plunge of his cock as if hypnotized. He thrust harder and I shrieked as he hit something inside me that felt like fireworks. My muscles clenched and strained against the tinsel.

Snick snick. The Christmas devil's claws sheared through the tinsel binding my ankles. Sighing with gratitude, I immediately raised my legs and spread them wide, changing the angle of my pelvis. Both Nicholas and I gasped as he sank even deeper into my welcoming heat.

My wrists were still bound and the tinsel was starting to cut into my flesh. The pain only added to the sensations overwhelming my nerves, coiling inside me like a cobra, my orgasm building and building for what seemed like an eternity.

"That pussy must be fucking amazing," Krampus said through clenched teeth, bending so his face hovered near mine. "I want a turn when you're done. When she's full of your cum I want to fuck it back inside her while you come down her throat." His long tongue snaked from his mouth and licked a path up my neck from my shoulder to my jaw.

The dirty words and his tongue against my skin made my pleasure spiral even higher. Nicholas looked like he wanted to chastise his friend but instead his thrusts became uneven, stuttering, his mouth falling open and his arms trembling, struggling to hold his torso over me while he climaxed.

"Look what you've done, you dirty Christmas whore," Krampus hissed in my ear. I knew I should hate the degrading way he spoke to me, but I loved it. It was everything I deserved, everything I wanted. "You're making Santa come in your filthy little cunt." Then he reached around and slid his free hand between my body and Nicholas's. He plucked at my clit like he was playing a guitar string.

That sent me over the edge, and then I was flying high, nerves electrified, the best orgasm of my life making me tremble and groan like a wild animal.

Nicholas collapsed on top of me and I went limp beneath him. I was vaguely aware of Krampus cutting my restraints, blood flooding back into my hands and making them burn. Then Krampus shoved Nicholas off me and pulled me to the edge of the bed. "My turn," he said, grinning down at me and lining up his huge cock with my entrance.

7

Peppermint and Eggnog

Nicholas body-checked him, knocking Krampus to the floor. "Give her a minute," he said, and turned to me. "Mädchen, do you need anything? Do you want to clean up?" He took my nearest ankle in his hands and massaged it gently.

I hadn't wanted to stop. I loved the image Krampus had painted of his big dick fucking another man's cum back into me, but I had to admit my mouth was dry and my hands and feet burned with pins and needles. "Water?"

Nicholas hurried out of the bedroom. Krampus got to his feet and approached me. I now lay at the edge of the bed where he'd left me, heart pounding, chest heaving. The devil grinned down at me. "Turn over, onto your hands and knees. Show me that gorgeous cunt."

Shivering, I obeyed, propping myself on hands and knees facing away from the goat-man, so I was looking at the headboard. It was agony on my stinging hands. Krampus stroked my ass and I winced, my flesh still sensitive from my earlier punishment. "Oh, poor little slut," Krampus crooned. Something cool and wet slid across my burning skin and it took me a moment to

33

realize it was his tongue lapping at my wounds. It felt good. Really, really good. I relaxed a little, letting my head hang down and my elbows bend until my forehead touched the mattress.

Nicholas returned to the bedroom. He hesitated in the doorway—I could hear his faltering steps against the carpet—but then came around the side of the bed and offered me the water glass. I tried to take it but my fingers weren't quite working yet, so Nicholas helped me drink awkwardly while Krampus continued licking my stinging ass cheeks. Nicholas eyed his companion warily.

Krampus stopped licking. "I want to fuck your dripping pussy, Noelle, while you suck Santa's cock. How does that sound?"

His words were like gasoline tossed on the fire of my lust. I turned to look at Nicholas, who was glaring at Krampus. His eyes slid back to mine and asked a silent question.

I nodded.

Krampus guffawed and gave my ass a happy slap. I squeaked at the pain.

Nicholas glared at his friend. "On one condition: no more spanking."

There was a pout in Krampus's voice when he said, "Aww. Killjoy."

And then something big and hard prodded at my pussy. Krampus sighed as he slid into me, the path already prepared by his whip handle and Nicholas's big cock. "So wet," he declared, grabbing my hips and pushing in to the hilt. "C'mon, alter Freund. Hurry up. I don't think I can hold back very long when her cunt feels this good."

I moaned; I couldn't help myself. It felt so good to be this full. I looked up at Nicholas, who was removing his boots and trousers with all due haste. He climbed onto the bed in front of me and presented me with his cock, which was already hard again. It was so beautiful, so big and slightly curved with a pulsing vein on one side, and smelled faintly of peppermint. I opened my mouth eagerly and he placed the head of it on my tongue.

Then Krampus coiled my long hair around one hand and yanked my head back so I was barely touching the mattress with my fingertips. He circled his hips, grinding his cock deep inside me, and I groaned at the sensation.

Relaxing his grip on my hair, Krampus let me fall forward until I was gagging on Nicholas's cock deep in my throat. Then, he roughly jerked me back so Nicholas's cock slid from my mouth. This brought me back onto the devil's cock, impaling me mercilessly. He did it again, and again, until the three of us had a rhythm going. I barely had to hold myself up—Krampus was doing most of the work for me—and I basked in the pleasure of being used so thoroughly. I let my muscles relax and pretended to be a sex doll, letting these men fuck me the way I'd always longed to be fucked.

I'd never really liked giving head, but this was something different. Two men using my mouth and my pussy simultaneously was apparently what I'd been missing all along. My pussy was full, and then my mouth. Then my pussy again. Krampus's dick slammed against my g-spot and then Nicholas's slammed against my gag reflex and somehow both were unbearably pleasurable. The sensations were so intense I almost felt like I was having an out-of-body experience, like this might finally be too much pleasure for one person to take. Krampus held me on Nicholas's cock longer each time, as if testing how long I could hold my breath. Could I die from too much sex? I decided, as I choked on hard flesh until tears poured down my face and sparks appeared in my vision, I was okay with dying right now if that was my fate.

Worth it.

"Oh, this pussy. I can see why you finished so early," Krampus told his friend through rasping breaths. "She feels so good. How's her mouth?"

Above me, Nicholas swallowed hard and managed to gasp, "Incredible."

"Well done, little slut," Krampus praised me. He stopped rocking me back and forth, settling me against his pelvis with his cock sheathed inside me. Then he started fucking me hard and fast, each thrust bumping my g-spot and making my tits jiggle obscenely. I screamed, another orgasm surging inside me. I pinched my own nipples as hard as I could, creating two bright pinpoints of pleasure.

Nicholas stared at my lower half, eyes wide. Krampus's free hand circled my waist and pressed to my abdomen. He laughed in his maniacal way when he thrust into me again. "I can feel myself inside you, Mädchen. I can feel my big cock wrecking your perfect pussy." His claws dug into my skin and I trembled and moaned in response.

How was it that every filthy, painful thing Krampus did or said made me feral with need? If anyone else had said these awful words to me, or done these brazen things, I would have made him regret it. But when Krampus did it, it was with such admiration and gratitude, as if he loved how wanton I was. "Slut" didn't feel like an insult when he used the word. And with Nicholas here to care for me and make sure his companion didn't go too far, I could truly let go and enjoy myself without fear or shame.

Nicholas pumped his cock a few times and hissed through his teeth, still staring at the place where the outline of Krampus's giant appendage must appear on my abdomen. His pleasure at the sight of his friend moving inside me made me feel like I was a wild animal just on the cusp of either climax or scratching my own eyes out.

"I don't think our friend can wait much longer," Krampus panted between thrusts. "We'd better come, don't you think, whore?" He pushed me down so my mouth was on Nicholas's cock again and leaned over my back, his tongue scoring my heated, sweaty flesh. "Come for us with one cock in your mouth and one in your cunt, being used the way a slut like you yearns for." And then he bit me, his sharp teeth sinking into my shoulder, and I shattered completely in a way I'd never experienced before, the power of the orgasm ripping through me and emptying my mind of every thought and my body of every sensation except pleasure so extreme my muscles gave out completely. Only Krampus's hand in my hair, teeth in my shoulder, and cock in my pussy held me up off the mattress.

Groaning, Nicholas clutched at my hair to hold my head in place and thrust into my mouth three times before coming down my throat. His cum tasted like peppermint. I swallowed it down, my throat working automatically.

When Nicholas flopped over onto the bed, spent, Krampus flipped me over in one swift motion. He pulled his cock from me and climbed onto the bed to straddle my waist, pumping himself above me until he groaned and came across my tits, just as he'd promised he would, in three hot spurts.

He sagged on top of me, sitting on my pelvis like I was a chair made for his comfort, big warm balls resting on my abdomen right where he'd touched me to feel his cock from the outside. He looked down at me with those alarming yellow eyes half-lidded in satisfaction, rapt, like he couldn't believe what he was looking at. Like he couldn't believe his luck.

Pride surged through me. Bossy Krampus was starry-eyed, at a loss for words, and Nicholas had collapsed onto the bed in a boneless heap. I'd done this to them. Sex with me, with my body, was so good I'd made these legends come all over me, inside and out.

The room smelled like sex, but also like peppermint and nutmeg. Curious, I reached down and collected a dollop of Krampus's cum on my finger. I brought it to my mouth and tasted it with the tip of my tongue. Krampus groaned at the sight, his long tongue unspooling to hang down his chin like he was an exhausted dog.

His cum tasted like eggnog.

8

Christmas Day

As soon as he was able to move again, Nicholas went to the bathroom and found a first aid kit. He insisted on cleaning and bandaging my bite wound and cursed at Krampus in that German-sounding language while he did it. Krampus, meanwhile, snuggled up behind me, one arm slung around my waist and his tail coiling around my calf. He gazed at the bite with a pleased expression while Nicholas cared for me.

I had no idea what to make of any of this. After so many orgasms, I could barely think at all.

Once the wound was clean and bandaged—and he'd smeared some kind of ointment onto my reddened ass cheeks—Nicholas stood and glanced at the door. He started gathering up his clothes.

"Nicholas?" I asked, the plea clear in my voice.

"I have a job to do," he said, his tone cold and professional. "We've wasted enough time."

"Don't be an ass," Krampus scolded him. "She needs more than just first aid after that. Get in the bed."

Nicholas sighed but obeyed, dropping the clothes and climbing onto the bed with us. It was only a queen mattress, and I ended up squished in between the two huge men, which was basically the greatest thing that had ever happened to me. I was surrounded by warmth, strength, and the smells of Christmas. It was everything I could ever ask for.

The grandfather clock downstairs chimed 12. It was midnight.

"Happy birthday, Noelle," Nicholas murmured into my hair, one of his hands gently stroking my hip.

"Happy birthday, Christmas slut," Krampus echoed, squeezing me tighter against him and peppering my neck with nips of his sharp teeth. His furry thighs pressed into mine and I peeked at three pairs of feet tangled together at the end of the bed, two human and one hooved. The sight made me giggle.

"This was the best birthday I've ever had," I whispered, and then drifted off to sleep in a warm, comfortable haze.

When I woke sometime later, the bed was cold and much too big. For a moment, I thought perhaps I'd imagined what happened the night before, but the scent of peppermint and nutmeg still lingered in the bedroom air and tinsel littered the tangled blankets. When I tried to get up, my entire body was sore, particularly my shoulder, where a bite mark large enough to be created by a huge dog was still fresh and raw. My pussy ached, but it was a good ache, and I hated how empty I felt now after being filled and used so well. The emptiness was punctuated by disappointment that my lovers had left without saying goodbye.

A thump drifted up from downstairs and adrenaline flooded me. They were still here! I rushed out of the room and down the stairs without dressing. Nicholas and Krampus stood beside the fireplace, Nicholas's big red bag slung over his shoulder and Krampus's whip coiled at his belt.

"You can't just leave me," I shouted, flinging myself at them.

Krampus caught me, crushing me against his chest. "Ah, Mädchen, you know we can't stay." He kissed the crown of my head.

"Then take me with you." The words escaped my mouth and I immediately wished I could pull them back in. I'd known these two men for mere hours. How desperate could a girl possibly be?

Claws dug into my hair at my nape and pulled my head back so I was staring up at Krampus, this myth of a man, this sadist satyr. "You don't want that. It's very lonely at the North Pole."

"I'm lonely here anyway. And the bank is about to foreclose on the house, so soon I'll have nowhere to live." I hadn't told anyone this, my greatest shame, but the words tumbled from me easily now, like our time together had knocked down the walls I'd built up around myself.

Krampus's expression softened a little. He reached into one of the pouches on his belt and removed something. He held it up for me to see before pressing it into my hand—a large gold coin. "So you can keep the house." He released me and stepped back.

"Th-thank you," I stuttered, staring bewildered at the coin. It was the size of a saucer and several times as heavy. "But I still want to go with you."

Nicholas stepped forward and cupped my jaw with one big hand. He looked into my eyes with his soulful blue irises, and I melted. "Noelle. Before you can go anywhere with us, you have amends to make, to others, and to yourself. If you truly want absolution, you know what to do." Then he kissed my forehead and stepped toward the fireplace.

Whoosh. He was gone.

"We'll be watching," Krampus said, a lascivious grin curling his mouth. His fangs glittered and his tongue lashed out to lick his lips suggestively. "It's up to you whether you're rewarded or punished next Christmas, hmm?" He winked, took a step back, and then *whooshed* up the chimney after his friend.

"Next Christmas?" I shouted after them. Did I have to wait until next Christmas to see them again? An entire year? Still holding the coin in one hand, I sank to the couch and listened to the clop of hooves and the jingle of bells as they left me.

Part of me wanted to cry and rage at the unfairness. Everybody left me, eventually. But wasn't that life? And anger wouldn't strictly be fair. They gave me a visit and stayed with me for hours. They granted my Christmas wish in ways I hadn't even foreseen. It was unfair to be angry they didn't take me with them—I hadn't asked for that in my wish. And Nicholas was right, I wasn't ready for it, either. A sensation of gratitude filled my chest, making my heart feel too big for my rib cage.

Now I had a year to make things right before they returned, to undo the hurt I'd caused and become a better person. And if I succeeded, maybe then they'd reward me by taking me with them to their home. Because even though I knew I'd miss my family, I still wanted to go. In my gut I knew without a doubt I belonged with Nicholas and Krampus. The North Pole couldn't possibly be a lonely place as long as the three of us were together.

Instead of lonely and sad, as I'd expected to feel, I was content and hopeful. "Happy birthday to me," I whispered, smiling at the chimney.

I decided to call my parents after I took a shower.

9

Letters

Dear Krampus and Nicholas,

Thanks to you, I got to spend Christmas and New Year with my family. When I called my parents on Christmas Day they invited me to come visit, so I took them up on that offer. It was an awkward week, but by the end of it, I felt like we'd gotten to know each other again. My mom remarked many times about how much I'd changed. I told her I have a new therapist. I wish I could have told her it was because of the two of you. She'd definitely think I was crazy if I did, though!

Then, also thanks to you, I paid all the late mortgage payments for the house and it's no longer in foreclosure. That coin was worth a lot, and it bought me the time I needed to find a job so I could start paying the mortgage payments myself. I applied for everything I could find, no matter the salary or the requirements. In the end, though, I got a job at a food bank sorting and packing boxes. I went there for food but came out with a job! It's boring and definitely doesn't make enough money to pay the bills, but it's a start. And I'm helping people, which feels good.

I dream of you at night, while I'm at work, in the shower, when I'm watching porn—basically all the time.

Love,

Noelle

A week after I mailed that letter, a response arrived. I knew it was from my North Pole lovers because the envelope was thick and luxurious, and my name and address were written in elegant calligraphy. Most telling of all, however, it smelled like peppermint.

Dear Noelle,

Your letter was a breath of warmth here in the cold. Don't tell Krampus I told you this, but we both miss you. He'd never admit it, but he calls out your name in his sleep, loud enough I can hear it from my room.

I've recruited some help making toys. It's still overwhelming, but not as bad as it was. I occasionally get to go for a sleigh ride just for fun, and it's less lonely having others around.

They're not you, though. I dream of your voice begging for me and the heat of your mouth.

We're proud of you.

Love,

Nicholas

The letter sustained me for weeks. Finally a small, discrete box arrived. When I opened it, there was a sex toy inside, a clitoral stimulator, and a gift note that said only:

Good girl. Use this and think of me.

–K

That night, and for many nights after, I did exactly as ordered. When I climaxed, I thought of Krampus between my legs, his long tongue thrashing against my clit, and Nicholas sucking my tits, his soft beard brushing my skin. Nicholas murmured praises while Krampus called me his Christmas slut. I burned candles with scents like Candy Cane Forest and Eggnog River so I could pretend they were in my home with me. I missed them fiercely, the way I'd never missed anyone before.

Dear Nicholas and Krampus,

Thank you for the gift. I'm enjoying it very much. I always thought Santa could see anyone he wants at any time, and I hope that's true, so you can enjoy the gift, also. I think of you both when I use it—and also the rest of the time. I think I might be obsessed. Sometimes I'm not sure whether I'm delusional but then I look at your letter and your note and I know you're real.

I contacted a former friend and apologized to her. She said there was nothing to apologize for and that she thought I was mad at her. So now we've cleared the air and we're speaking again. Much like with my family, I'm not sure she trusts me quite yet, but that's okay. We'll get there.

I've stopped drinking and started doing yoga. I'm doing both for you, because I know you want me to take care of myself. I do feel better since quitting booze, but the jury is still out on the yoga. It makes me sore in places I didn't even know had muscles, but I'm also getting stronger and my balance is getting better.

With all my heart,

Noelle

In response to this letter, I received another box. This one was large and contained yoga pants in my size, a yoga mat, and a water bottle. The note accompanying the gifts said:

I want you so flexible I can put your feet behind your head.

–K

The note made me laugh, but it also made my pussy flood with wetness and clench on nothing. Krampus was such a lech, but I loved it. For weeks after this note, I masturbated to the mental image of him bending me in half like a folding chair and fucking me senseless.

A few days later, a longer letter arrived from Nicholas.

Dear Noelle,

Krampus is becoming increasingly cranky here at the North Pole. We both miss you, but you'd think someone killed his puppy by the way he rages around here. I've never seen him like this before. I'm trying to find a way for us to come visit you before Christmas so I won't have to kick him out.

My helpers continue to be useful. We're making gifts at record speed. I'm not accustomed to having people around, though. The helpers love Christmas, which is great, but they want to play Christmas music all day every day, which is less great. I love Christmas, too, but that Mariah Carey song makes me want to lay down in the snow and let the reindeer run me over.

I won't, though. Not if there's a chance I might see you again.

Love,

Nicholas

Naturally, I wrote back.

Dear Krampus and Nicholas,

Thank you for the yoga gear and your letter. I miss you, too. I hope you can find a way to visit before Christmas, but be assured that I'm fine, and I'll wait for you forever, if I have to.

Love,

Noelle

I tucked several photos of myself in with the letter. In the photos, I'm doing yoga poses in lingerie. I imagined their reactions when they saw the pictures for the first time and grinned when I put the envelope in the mail. I'd never been brave enough to take sexy photos of myself and send them to a boyfriend like this, but it felt easy with Nicholas and Krampus. Easy and safe. I had a feeling Krampus would rather rip another man's eyes out than let them look at me, and Nicholas was probably the most trustworthy man on Earth.

Were they my boyfriends? It was a thrilling idea, but the word didn't feel adult enough. I preferred "lovers." I didn't tell anyone about them, but people noticed anyway. My friends and family commented on my newfound confidence. I actually wanted to get out of bed every morning, if only to check the mail for correspondence. I caught myself smiling a lot more.

And my anger was gone, replaced with a new surety that everything was going to be okay.

10

The Night Before Easter

In April the snow finally melted and the temperatures warmed. Part of me was grateful for nicer weather and part of me was sad to leave winter behind. Winter was the season of Christmas, the season when I met the men I love.

Love. It was weird to think I might love Krampus and Nicholas. I knew logically I was probably just infatuated, but tell my heart that.

I got a promotion at work. It was just enough money to pay my bills but came with a lot more responsibility. I didn't write to my lovers as much as I should have. I barely managed to get in yoga practice most days. I felt good, accomplished, like I was turning my life around, but also like something was missing. I knew what it was, but I had no way of getting it. Getting *them*.

Maybe, I started to think, I should let go of Krampus and Nicholas. Living without them 364 days a year was wearing on me. It had only been three months and I was already lonely. Could I do this forever? I let myself imagine having a relationship with an ordinary man, or at least visiting a swinger's club to take the edge off, but when I looked around at the men at work, at yoga, and on the street, none of them appealed to me. How could they? Their competition was a 7-foot-tall demon and hot, tattooed Santa Claus, both with giant dicks and talented mouths. Nobody would ever compare. I'd been ruined for anyone else.

Easter was on April 20th. On the 19th, in the wee hours of the morning, a sound woke me from a deep sleep. I strained in the darkness for more sounds that might indicate intruders, but heard nothing else, so I rolled over to go back to sleep.

A big, warm hand settled around my throat and a hot, wet tongue licked its way up the side of my neck and face. "Good morning, Mädchen." The scent of nutmeg surrounded me.

Fear was immediately replaced with disbelief and then excitement. "Krampus?" I twisted in his grip so I could see him. He smiled down at me, huge and hideous, like something out of a nightmare, and my heart thumped a staccato beat that was only for him.

The lamp in the corner clicked on and illuminated Nicholas, leaning against the wall and smiling under his thick beard. "Hello, Noelle. Happy Easter."

"How did you get here?" I asked. Without another word, Krampus yanked down the blankets and pushed up the oversize t-shirt I'd worn to bed. I grabbed his horns as he sucked on my right nipple while his clawed fingers pinched the left one, sending lightning bolts of pleasure through my body that brought me to alertness faster than a cup of coffee.

"The Easter Bunny owed me a favor," Nicholas said, grinning.

"So you're just here for tonight?" I gasped against Krampus's fangs and claws.

"Unfortunately," Nicholas said.

"So we need to make the most of it," Krampus growled. He

hooked his fingers under the waistband of my panties and ripped them from my body. Thank goodness they were an ugly old pair of granny panties I wore only for sleeping. He spread my knees and made a satisfied hiss when I was bared to him. "I've missed this little cunt." And then he dove in head-first with his usual gusto.

"I can't believe you're here," I said to Nicholas between moans. I reached for him and he walked over to the bed to take my hand. Then he lifted my shoulders and slid beneath me so my head rested in his lap.

He leaned in and kissed me tenderly, which was quite the contrast with Krampus nipping my clit and sliding a knuckle inside my slick pussy. Nicholas placed his hands over my breasts and played with my nipples. "You're glad to see us, then?"

I moaned as Krampus's tongue flicked inside me and then rolled over my clit. "It's all I've wanted since Christmas day."

Krampus lifted his mouth from me long enough to say, "I told you so. She can't get enough of our cocks, can you, slut?"

In response I whimpered and rolled my hips. I was on the precipice of orgasm already. "Fuck me please, sir."

Krampus's yellow eyes flashed with pleasure. He liked being called "sir." Good. I liked calling him that.

"How do you want it, Mädchen?"

"I want your cock." My voice was breathy with desire.

"Do you want to look at me while I fuck you? Or do you want me from behind?"

"I want to look at you." The words came out shrill with desperation.

"Do you want it hard and fast or slow and gentle?"

We should have probably taken it slow, as I hadn't had a dick inside me in months, but that wasn't what I wanted. "Hard, please, sir. Please punish me."

"Better not make her wait any longer," Nicholas said, pushing my hair back from my face. "She's already about to explode." He slid off the bed and moved away.

Krampus shifted, climbing up the bed until he loomed over me. He was truly massive, a great horned shadow in the dim light. His huge cock stood at attention, hard and ready. This was going to hurt, but I still longed for it. Longed for *him*. He slid his hands under my hips and his claws pricked my skin as he positioned me just so, and then stabbed himself inside me with one sharp thrust of his hips.

I screamed, but not with pain. He felt incredible. His cock split me open, filled me up, made me whole. My nerves sang with pleasure. I reached up and grabbed his horns, forcing his head down toward me so I could stare into those big yellow eyes of his with the rectangular goat pupils I once found so unnerving. Now, they were just part of him, just another part I'd come to love.

His long black tongue flicked out and circled my nipples one at a time. He closed his eyes like he was relishing every sensation. When he opened them again, they were yellow slits that seemed to bore into my soul with their intensity. His hot breath on my face smelled like chocolate and marshmallows. "Are you ready?"

I nodded, and he flexed his hips, withdrawing from me slowly, and then slammed back in so far I swear the head of his dick stabbed my spine. Then he began doing exactly as I'd asked, and pounded into me like a jackhammer. His huge hands gripped my buttocks, holding me in place so he could angle each thrust until he found just the right spot. When he did, fireworks filled my vision and every muscle in my body clenched. I closed my eyes and tipped my head back, screaming through a powerful orgasm.

"Yes, yes, that's it Mädchen, my Christmas whore. Come for me," Krampus drawled, and followed this with a string of words in that guttural language of his I didn't understand. He buried his face in my neck and his wet tongue slithered against the scars left by his teeth, tracing them while he thrust into me faster and harder.

He grabbed one of my legs and pushed it up over his shoulder, somehow making it possible for him to fuck me even deeper. His tail wound around my other leg and pressed the back of my thigh to the bed. The sight of him burying his cock in me with my foot against his neck was so erotic another orgasm started to tingle up my spine. "Yes, sir, yes," I gasped. "Put your cum in me." My hands went to his chest and I curled my fingers into his soft fur.

The Christmas devil's grin was lecherous as he reached down and flicked my clit. This second climax hit me like a truck, making my whole body shudder and a howl erupt from my throat. Krampus tipped his head back and his thrusts became erratic. He grunted a few times and then wet heat flooded my insides.

Panting hard, Krampus collapsed on top of me. He was big and heavy and for a moment I was scared he might crush me, but somehow he didn't. A miracle of Christmas magic, I guess. His arms went around me and pulled me to his chest while his tongue went back to tracing the marks of his teeth on the skin of my shoulder. I sunk my hands into his fur, trying to memorize the way his body felt against mine, the softness of his pelt, the texture of his horns, the sensation of his hot, wet tongue against my shoulder, the fullness of his cock stuffed inside me, the way his claws gently prickled against my skin without breaking it.

Gradually his breathing slowed and his tongue returned to his mouth. He released me and withdrew his cock. Hot wetness dripped from my pussy down to my ass and the scent of eggnog filled the room.

Krampus crawled off me and crumpled onto the other half of the bed like a plushy whose stuffing had been yanked out. One of his big hands settled on my thigh, a furry lead weight, while his tail remained coiled around my ankle, stroking gently.

Nicholas appeared with a glass of water and helped me sit up to drink a few sips. He laughed at my boneless flopping as he practically carried me to the bathroom to use the toilet. Then he helped me back to the bed. While his arm was around me, I leaned into him and breathed deep of his peppermint scent. It was instantly soothing.

He lowered me back to the bed. "What about you?" I asked, reaching for his belt.

He smiled. "I'm fine." He nodded at his companion, who was now snoring softly. "That's the best he's slept in months."

I unlatched Nicholas's belt and slid off the bed to kneel in front of him. "Don't be silly. You came all this way."

"You don't have to," he said, stroking my hair with his big, callused hands. "It's enough just to see you."

I pulled down his pants until his cock was free, springing up big and hard right in front of my face. "But I want to," I said, licking the soft head. He gasped and I grinned. There was power in having this effect on a man, especially *this* man.

I kissed the velvety skin of the head first, and then moved down the shaft, licking and kissing and enjoying the mixture of musk and mint that filled my senses. Finally I opened my mouth and slowly descended on his cock, taking it as deep as I could, until it hit the back of my throat and I nearly gagged.

Nicholas let out a grunt. His fingers curled in my hair, gripping the strands hard enough to make my scalp sting. I moaned with my mouth around him and his hips bucked. "Ah, Noelle," he sighed, holding my head in place so he could gently thrust into my mouth. "Ah, your sweet mouth."

Tears rose in my eyes and my pussy gushed as he fucked my face. I put my hands on his ass, pulling him deeper into my mouth and humming as I did it, swirling my tongue against the tip of his cock.

Suddenly he jerked back, releasing me and withdrawing his cock from my mouth. "What's wrong?" I asked.

"I don't want to cum in your mouth," he said. He reached down and lifted me by the armpits until I was standing.

"I don't mind." In fact, a part of me was looking forward to the hot peppermint flavor on my tongue.

"I want to watch your face while I fuck you," he admitted.

I grinned and let him hoist me up to his waist, closing my legs around him. In a few wobbly steps, he took us to the wall beside the bathroom door and pressed me against it so he could kiss me with three months' worth of pent-up passion. I grabbed the hem of his shirt and helped him pull it over his head, revealing his muscular torso. His tattooed body was just as beautiful as I remembered.

We adjusted our bodies until his cock slid between my lower lips and nestled against my clit, hard and warm and throbbing. He groaned as he pushed it against me. "You're so wet." I almost climaxed just from the feeling of his body against mine. He wasn't even inside me yet and I didn't think I'd last much longer.

"I like it when you fuck my face," I admitted, threading my fingers through his hair at the nape of his neck and bringing his face close so I could kiss him. We explored each others' mouths, tongues tangling. I combed my fingers through his soft beard and ran my hands through his hair until the leather tie holding it back gave way and his long, white mane tumbled out and around his shoulders.

"God you're beautiful," I whispered.

Nicholas flushed. "You're the beautiful one." And then he rocked his hips back and forward and sank into me.

He was much more gentle than Krampus had been and my sore pussy appreciated it. He fucked me slowly and with care, pinching my nipples and circling my clit with his thumb until I came, stars bursting behind my eyelids and my back arching against the wall. He moved inside me faster until I was bouncing on his cock, tits jiggling, whimpering at the wonderful sensation of his dick against my g-spot. I grabbed his ass cheeks and pulled him into me as deep as he would go, so deep I could practically taste his peppermint cum when he finally lost himself to orgasm and pumped me full of liquid heat.

I was so full I could feel his cum dripping out of me around his softening erection. But still I wanted more, more, knowing it might be months before I could have him again. They could fill me to bursting and it would never be enough.

He carried me to the bed without withdrawing his cock from my pussy and lowered us both carefully onto the mattress, trying not to wake his sleeping friend. He didn't pull out; instead, he started kissing me, playing with my breasts, reaching down and stroking my clit, until I moaned and felt him harden inside me again. He rolled us over until I was on top, riding him, and we made love that way, staring into each others' eyes, whispering and whimpering and rolling our hips until we both came again.

Krampus snored through all of it.

11

Easter Morning

I woke to something sliding between my legs and a pair of huge hands massaging my breasts. I must have rolled off Nicholas in the night, because he lay on his side in front of me, eyes closed, breaths deep and steady.

Behind me, Krampus prodded at my sore pussy with his enormous cock while something—his tail?—stroked my clit. His long tongue licked at his favorite spot, the bite mark on my shoulder.

I knew I should say no and push him away, but how could I? Just as with Nicholas, this was my only chance to get my fill of him for what could be months. So I opened my legs just enough that he could slide his cock between them and against my entrance.

Krampus rocked gently, easing himself inside me in sharp contrast to his earlier impatient thrusting. His tail and tongue and hands all worked at me until I was panting with desire, my body relaxed enough for him to fit himself inside the place he belonged without pain.

"Ah, Mädchen. Do you like waking up being fucked like the

good slut you are?" He whispered in my ear.

"Yes," I admitted. This was way better than any alarm clock.

He froze, halting all movement, and I squeaked in protest. "Yes, what?" he coaxed.

"Yes, sir."

He chuckled, his hot breath against my neck making me tingle and writhe, and started moving again. "Good girl."

It felt like his cock was never ending, the way more of it kept sliding into me with each rock of his hips. Just when I thought he was surely seated all the way inside me, he'd push in just a little more, until I was so full I didn't think I could take any more. But then, by some miracle, I would, like my insides were shaped to fit him, and he only needed to remind them of this fact.

It was hard to hold back sounds of pleasure as he filled me in the best way possible. One of Krampus's big hands came up and covered my mouth so we wouldn't wake Nicholas.

I whimpered and moaned into his hand until finally, finally I felt his hips flush with my ass. Then he slowly withdrew, taking his time, letting us both enjoy the sensation of his hard cock dragging along the soft walls of my pussy.

"Ah, this magical cunt of yours," he sighed. "I'll never get enough."

I wanted to tell him I felt the same way about his cock, his tongue, his filthy mouth, but all I could do was groan against his palm and squeeze the walls of my pussy around him, hoping he understood.

He pushed back in, the leisurely motion of his hips making me twitch and whimper, desperate for speed and friction. I clutched at his hands, one over my mouth and the other plucking and pinching each of my nipples in turn, while his tail rubbed my clit, filling me with need, driving me to the precipice of orgasm.

Holding me so tight I could barely move, Krampus fucked me like that for what felt like hours, until I thought I might pass out. Nicholas lay less than a foot away, sleeping contentedly, while his companion whispered the filthiest words I'd ever heard into my ear and shoved his cock in so deep his furry balls brushed the backs of my thighs. It was agony and ecstasy. I wanted him to hurry up and fuck me and make me come until I saw stars, but I also never wanted this slow torture to end.

Krampus's tail flicked against my clit and I twitched violently, making the whole bed shake. Nicholas opened his eyes and regarded me, wrapped up in Krampus, impaled on his friend's massive cock, and cracked a smile.

"Good morning, Noelle."

Krampus moved his hand so I could speak. "It's not morning yet," I croaked, throat dry. "Still dark outside."

"Do you want to join us, alter Freund?" Krampus inquired. He tried to make it sound casual, but the strain in his voice was unmistakable. He was coming undone by his own slow, agonizing ministrations, and I felt strangely triumphant. He wanted to be the one in control, but I was destroying that control without even trying.

"Looks like you've got it covered," Nicholas said. "I'll just watch." He took his cock in his hand—already erect, just from seeing me and Krampus like this—and stroked it lazily. His eyes went to my abdomen and he bit his lower lip at what he saw there. That's how I knew Krampus's cock must be outlined against my skin again, making my stomach bulge each time he thrust back inside me.

Nicholas watching made everything that much hotter. I whimpered, gripping Krampus's furry arms, and rolled my hips to urge him to speed up.

"Do you want me to fuck you properly now that Nicholas is watching?" Krampus asked.

I nodded. His hand went to my throat, holding me in place, and he snapped his hips so he thrust inside me so abruptly and so deep a yelp startled from my lips. He snarled in my ear as he withdrew and did it again, and again, until I was crying with pleasure, tears streaking down my face and onto my pillows. Each stab of his cock against my g-spot was like a mini orgasm in itself, a pleasure so intense it was hard to stay conscious.

The flicking of his tail against my clit sped up, winding me up tighter, and his fingers pinched my nipples brutally. The orgasm hovered just out of reach. I strained against him, every muscle tensed, desperate for release.

Nicholas leaned in and kissed me, his free hand going to my available breast, and I was undone. I screamed into his mouth as the orgasm racked my body, wringing me out. I twitched and jerked long after it was over, as Krampus continued to thrust, one hand pressed to my abdomen as if he, too, loved the cock-bulge we'd created, the writhing of his tail against my clit becoming sloppy and unfocused.

"Ah my Christmas slut, my angel," he growled, his hips slamming into me with wet smacks. "You feel so good, your perfect cunt, you're so tight and so wet."

"Come for me, sir," I whispered.

At last, he did, roaring his release to the ceiling. His cum spurted inside me hot as lava and his body jerked and shuddered with the force of his orgasm. Even as he filled me, however, he was careful not to clench his fist around my throat.

And that's how I realized Krampus loved me.

"Are you alright?" Nicholas asked, sweeping strands of hair back from my sweaty face as Krampus released me.

I could only nod, panting too hard to make words. Nicholas found the glass of water from earlier and helped me sit up to drink the rest of it. Then he and Krampus tucked me between them once again, the bed too full, our feet tangled up with each others' and the blankets. I thought about getting a bigger bed, but then I thought, no. I won't be staying here past the end of the year.

I was definitely going to the North Pole this Christmas.

12

The Long Wait

Nicholas and I wrote back and forth regularly after Easter. Letters of longing and love, words of passion and lust. He wrote poetry so beautiful it made me cry. He poured his heart into descriptions of the parts of me he missed the most, especially my eyes. I started to see how women fell in love with men through letters back before the telephone was invented.

Krampus, meanwhile, sent me a bouquet of dildos with a note: "For when you miss me." I laughed and used them with the lights on and the blankets thrown back. I hoped the song was right and they could see me when I was sleeping, and when I was awake.

There were no more holidays between Easter and Christmas when they could visit. It was a long and lonely seven months, but I turned down every guy who asked me on a date. I told them I was taken. I spent a lot of time alone and began to enjoy it, if I'm honest. I took up knitting, figuring it would keep my hands and mind busy and maybe even prove useful if I moved to the North Pole.

I taught myself to bake, also, and gained weight. I fretted that my lovers wouldn't like my new curves but Krampus sent me a box of cookies just to make sure I knew he didn't care.

The cookies were eggnog flavor, and I ate every single one.

I made sure to enjoy every moment with my friends and family. I didn't intend to see them again after my birthday that year because I wanted to go home with my lovers. I tried not to get my hopes up about it, but I couldn't help myself. What would I do if Nicholas said no? I had a feeling, despite his earlier protests, Krampus would be happy to take me home and keep me as a sex slave in the dungeon I felt certain was his room. But Nicholas might hesitate, worried I'd feel both lonely and trapped at the North Pole.

I think that's how he felt about living there, and he didn't want anyone else he cared about to feel the same.

As Christmas approached, I found myself knitting two pairs of extra large mittens and watching every Christmas movie on every streaming service. I was disappointed the only Krampus movie I could find was a horror film, but I still watched it three times, and masturbated after. Can you blame me? I was so horny, even wildly inaccurate horror movie Krampus looked good.

That's around the time when, to my delight, I discovered Krampus erotica. I started mailing the books to the North Pole with the wildest passages highlighted. The Krampus in the books wasn't always accurate, but the books were often hilarious, and certainly good enough to distract me from missing my guys.

I could hardly believe it when Christmas Eve finally arrived. On the morning of the 24th, I found a package on my front doorstep. It contained a set of red lingerie in my size and nothing else. Not even a note or a gift receipt.

But I knew who it was from. I pressed my thighs together in

anticipation and immediately went to try it on.

13

Christmas Eve (Encore)

I finished wrapping the last of the gifts for my family and chose a Christmas movie to watch while I waited. Curled up under a blanket on my sofa, I sipped from a glass of eggnog (the non-alcoholic kind) and smiled at the memories it brought flooding back.

Sometimes I nearly convinced myself I must have imagined everything, but all I had to do was reach up and trace the bite marks in my shoulder and I knew the wild nights with Krampus and Nicholas had been real. I kept Nicholas's letters, too, and the little notes Krampus included with his gifts. Of course, I could have written those myself in an effort to prove my delusion, but the teeth marks would be much harder to fake. When I touched them, my flesh hummed with the memory. It was like Krampus had left his mark on me to make sure I'd remember.

I also had the lingerie, which I was wearing under my favorite giant t-shirt.

I went to the kitchen to refill my eggnog. With the movie paused, the night was quiet and peaceful.

A sound from above startled me. It sounded like...bells? It was quickly followed by the *clop* of hooves on my roof.

My pulse picked up. Tears of relief rose in my eyes as I dropped the carton of eggnog on the counter and ran for the living room.

Krampus and Nicholas already stood there, as if they'd thrown themselves down the chimney before the sleigh had even stopped moving. Nicholas's face was obscured by the hood of his scarlet coat, but Krampus grinned at me, white fangs flashing and yellow eyes burning like two bright lanterns.

"Krampus," I sighed, unable to stop grinning. "Nicholas! You're here."

"We are," Krampus confirmed. His tongue lashed the air like he was tasting it, and his tail coiled itself around the leg of my coffee table as if it had a mind of its own.

"I have mulled cider in the crock pot, if you're thirsty." I gestured awkwardly to the kitchen.

"We're not here for drinks," Krampus said, that wicked grin still splitting his face.

I exhaled and it came out shaky. My heart galloped. "Then why did you come?"

Nicholas lowered his hood. He was just as stunning as I remembered, even if it was too dark in my living room for me to see the color of his eyes. "We came for you, of course."

A lump surged up my throat and I started sobbing, relief and joy overwhelming me. Nicholas pulled me into his warm embrace. The smell of gingerbread and candy canes enveloped me. "You came back," I sobbed, by way of explanation. "You actually came back. I started to think maybe I imagined everything."

Nicholas held me tightly and pressed a kiss into my hair. "I'm sorry we couldn't visit again. The rules of Christmas magic are strict."

"No Halloween King to bring you in October?" I smiled up at

him through my tears.

"Krampus bit him once," Nicholas admitted with a rueful expression.

Krampus snorted. "He deserved it."

That made me laugh, and both men grinned down at me, and suddenly I was crying, and two pairs of strong arms—and a tail—were wrapped around me.

"You've outdone yourself on the decorations," Nicholas commented, gazing around my little house. I'd strung garlands from the ceiling. The new Christmas tree was twice the size of the old one and decorated with so much tinsel and so many ornaments the branches sagged. Most of my life I'd resented Christmas because it was also my birthday, but I'd become an unbridled Christmas enthusiast in the last twelve months.

Krampus grinned again, yellow eyes sparkling. "Tinsel." He placed one giant, clawed hand at my waist and used the other to drag down the collar of my sweater. His long tongue swiped across the scar of his bite mark on my shoulder. "You missed us, didn't you, little Christmas slut?"

Gasping at the touch of his claws and tongue and the filthiness of his words, I nodded and hid my face against Nicolas's chest.

"Still so shy," Krampus crooned, his breath hot on my neck. "But Krampus always knows what his whore wants most. I think your Christmas wish must be the same as mine, Mädchen." His tail coiled around my leg and slid up my thigh under my t-shirt to tease me, swiping at the gusset of the red panties.

I shivered. "What wish is that?"

"For you to come home with us."

My heart stopped, time frozen.

"Do you want to?" Nicholas asked, his voice barely above a whisper, as if he were afraid of the answer. "It's pretty cold and lonely. You might get bored—"

"Stop trying to convince her not to come!" Krampus roared.

I nodded and dashed tears from my eyes. "Of course I want to come with you." My voice was choked, my limbs trembling. Was my dream really coming true?

"What about your family?" Nicholas asked.

"Who cares?" Krampus asked, scowling. "She made her Christmas wish and now we must honor it. Let's go."

"Would you shut up?" Nicholas snapped. "You wanted me to do this and—"

"I didn't want you to do anything! I thought we should just throw her in the sleigh and I still think that."

"Her consent is important."

"Will you two stop arguing?" I interjected, sniffling and biting back a laugh. "You're like two cranky grandfathers in a nursing home."

"Hot grandfathers, though." Krampus's frown transformed back into that lascivious grin I was coming to know very well.

"What I was trying to say, Noelle, before we were interrupted," Nicholas said, glaring at Krampus for an instant before turning back to me, "Is that, if you're sure you want to, we'd like you to come home with us."

"For how long?" I asked. I couldn't believe this was happening. Was it a hallucination? I reached up and touched Nicholas's jaw, but he was solid, his skin warm under my fingers, his beard thick and soft. This was real.

Nicholas smiled and it was so gentle, so hopeful. "However long you like."

"Preferably forever," Krampus barked. "It's someone else's turn to entertain this old fart."

I nodded again. "I spent this year making amends to all the

people I hurt and trying to become a better person. And I learned to knit, and bake. All so I could come with you."

Nicholas smiled down at me with such open joy I felt like I was drowning in it, but in a good way. "It really is cold and lonely, and you can only visit your family at Christmas."

Krampus snorted and strode forward, tugging me from his companion's arms and throwing me over his shoulder in a fireman's carry. "Enough talking." He planted a firm slap on my backside that made me yelp. "She said yes. Stop trying to convince her to change her mind and get in the goddamn sleigh."

An instant later, we were somehow on the rooftop and Krampus was dropping me into the seat of a wide sleigh pulled by eight huge reindeer.

"Krampus!" I shouted, half-laughing. "You have to stop doing that! You can't just throw me in the sleigh like I'm a sack of potatoes."

The sky was clear and the moon was nearly full, limning the world in silver. Krampus loomed over me, arms crossed over his chest. "You want to come with us, yes?"

I struggled to get to my feet. At the front of the sleigh, the reindeer pawed the roof of my house impatiently. I swallowed hard and sat back down, viscerally reminded that I was afraid of heights when the world spun around me. "Yes, but—"

Krampus bent down and hissed in my ear, "Then be a good little slut and do as you're told."

My response was to shiver, both with cold and with desire. Krampus grinned. I hated that he knew exactly what to say to get me to obey, but I also loved it.

So much for the mittens I'd made them.

Nicholas swung up into the seat beside me and grabbed the reins. "Ready? Hold on."

"Oh, god," I groaned, burying my face in Nicholas's coat and throwing my arms around his waist.

The sensation of the sleigh rising was much like that of a plane taking off, only much jerkier and quicker. My stomach did somersaults for a few seconds, but then we were airborne, and suddenly the flight was as smooth as any plane trip I'd ever taken. I peeked out from behind the Nicholas's coat to see the stars whizzing past as the reindeer traveled with impossible, magical speed. I didn't dare look down, but I knew with certainty I was up very, very high as clouds parted for the sleigh.

"Where exactly are we going?" I asked. I was surprised to find my voice wasn't ripped away by the wind, and I wasn't cold like I should be, either.

"Our home," Nicholas told me, draping an arm around my shoulders and hugging me close to his body.

I was surprised I could hear him over the whoosh of the wind and the jingling of the harness bells on the reindeer. I should have been cold, too, but I wasn't.

Krampus slid across the seat until his huge, furry thigh touched mine. He bent his head down toward me and I got a whiff of whipped cream and cloves. "Have you ever been fucked in a flying sleigh, Mädchen?"

"N–no."

He grinned. "Would you like to be?"

My entire body flushed, my nipples hardening. I couldn't manage words, but I nodded.

14

The Sleigh

Krampus lowered himself onto the floor of the sleigh and maneuvered until he was in front of me. It was awkward, and I had a sneaking suspicion someone was using some Christmas magic to make his huge body fit in the narrow space. Then he ran his clawed hands up the inside of my thighs and licked his lips. His golden eyes flashed when he pushed the t-shirt up and got a look at what I was wearing underneath.

"Good girl," he crooned, running one clawed finger along the lacy red panties he'd sent me.

His eyes met mine, asking a silent question. I nodded again and bit my lip in anticipation. He grabbed the hem of the giant t-shirt and ripped it off over my head. Then, as if he couldn't help himself, he yanked off the pretty scarlet panties, baring my pussy to the air. He pressed the crotch of the fabric to his nose, inhaling deeply, before casting the clothes onto the floor of the sleigh.

Krampus pushed my knees apart and gazed almost reverently upon me. "I've waited so long for this, Mädchen. Your cunt is just as beautiful as I remember."

His long tongue slipped from his mouth and anticipation made me tremble. Something pinched my nipple and I realized Nicholas's hand had slid around my shoulder and now cupped one of my tits. He rolled my nipple between his fingers and kissed my hair while he watched Krampus lashing me with his tongue, working my clit and fucking me with the length of it until I was moaning and writhing and my wetness glistened in the moonlight.

Then the monster stood, returning to his seat, and lifted me by my waist in one smooth motion to impale me on his massive cock. I'd had nothing to prepare me this time, and the intrusion was both painful and blissful. I screamed into the night air and Krampus made a pleased sound deep in his throat.

"There we are, that's where my cock belongs. Buried in this magical cunt," Krampus said, his low voice full of gravel.

I slid down his shaft inch by delectable inch until I was seated fully on the devil's lap. He reached up to pull my breasts from the cups of the lingerie. His tongue swirled around my tits and up my neck, and then he kissed me for the first time. His mouth was too big and it was a little awkward, but his lips were surprisingly soft, and his fangs scraped at my lips just enough to add an edge of danger. My whole body shuddered in pleasure and my pussy clenched around him.

I was so wonderfully full. I wanted to start rocking, to find the friction I longed for, but Krampus held my hips down so I could only grind against him in frustration.

It was then I became aware that Nicholas had gotten up and stepped behind me. He massaged my tits with his big, rough hands, pinching and twisting my nipples until I whimpered. He kissed my jaw, my neck, and my naked shoulder, leaving blooms of pleasure wherever his lips touched.

"He won't let me come," I whined to Nicholas over my shoulder.

He chuckled. "Don't worry, Noelle, you'll always get to come." He kissed me passionately, our tongues tangling until I was breathless.

I felt something prodding the entrance to my already full pussy and groaned. Was he serious? I was already so full of Krampus I could burst, and now Nicholas wanted to jam his enormous cock in there, too? It wasn't possible. They'd rip me in half!

Christmas magic must have worked again, because Nicholas's hard cock slid inside me. Krampus and I both groaned as he entered. For a few long seconds, all three of us held completely still, bodies adjusting. I'd never felt so full in my life. The sensation was almost more than I could bear and the instant Krampus removed his hands from my hips I started rocking.

"Ah, ah, yes, that's it, what a good girl," Krampus panted.

"You feel incredible," Nicholas groaned in my ear. "This is *incredible.*"

It forgot I was in a sleigh, rocketing through the cold night air while the world slept beneath me. I forgot about everything except my lovers, and this moment, flesh on flesh, breath on breath. Pressed between them, both of them inside me, felt like where I belonged.

I kissed them each in turn while I rocked and they thrust, and we came to a rhythm that worked for all three of us. I clutched at Krampus, who gripped my ass with his clawed fingers. Nicholas held onto my tits as he rocked into me and out. We all moaned and whimpered together with each thrust. I had never experienced anything so magnificent.

Krampus licked at the wound on my shoulder possessively and I tilted my head to give him better access. Something soft and sinuous circled my throat—Krampus's tail, applying just enough pressure I could feel it restricting my breath without squeezing so tightly I lost consciousness. I locked eyes with the Christmas devil and he grinned, relishing my fear, enjoying the way I let him use my body with total abandon. His pleasure only ratcheted mine higher and I dug my nails into his biceps and groaned.

Nicholas dropped a hand between us and found my clit. "Fuck, you're so wet," he gasped, his fingers sliding against my slick flesh.

"You're so hard," I mewled. "I can't take much more."

"Come for us, Mädchen," Nicholas hissed.

"Come on our cocks, slut," Krampus added, his tail tightening on my throat.

I let go at last, stars exploding in my vision. My body shuddered and jerked as the orgasm seemed to pinch every nerve I had. The two men continued fucking me, their rhythm becoming frantic, until Nicholas wrapped his arms around me to hold me in place and thrust himself home.

"Ah! Noelle." He came so hard he dropped to his knees on the floor of the sleigh after it was over, babbling something in that language I couldn't understand. I made a mental note to have them teach me this language of theirs. We'd have plenty of time for it.

While Nicholas climbed, panting, up into the seat to take the reigns again, Krampus grasped me by the hips and used me like a sex doll, thrusting into me hard and fast while lifting and dropping me onto his cock. Practically boneless, I couldn't stop him. I didn't want to stop him. I loved being used by him, loved being fucked like a toy. My mind was blissfully clear and my only thought was that I wanted this to last forever.

He was right; I'd become a complete slut for him. It should have been a shocking thought but instead it made sense in a way that made me feel as if I were whole and complete for the first time. I didn't need to feel shame over my desires because they were meant for these men, these two perfect men, one a sadist and the other a gentle giant, both wonderful in their own way. This was what I'd always been missing.

Finally, Krampus slammed into me one last time and roared his orgasm to the world. Inside me, his cock twitched and spurted for a few long seconds. I went limp on his chest, breathing hard, worn out like I'd just run a marathon. The scents of sweat and gingerbread clung to us.

Krampus gathered me in his arms and stroked my back with his claws, murmuring words of praise. His cock softened inside me and slid from my pussy, followed by a gush of his and Nicholas's combined fluids. I shivered. The open air was chilly on my cooling skin.

Nicholas wrapped his furred cloak around me and pulled me into his lap. Floating in a post-sex haze, I barely noticed the sleigh slowing to a halt and Nicholas carrying me somewhere. Krampus stroked my hair with one clawed hand.

"Welcome home, Noelle," Nicholas said, kissing my forehead.

I, sighed, closed my eyes, and snuggled into his coat that smelled like Christmas morning.

15

Epilogue

Nicholas's voice was smooth and deep like fancy liqueur, sliding across my skin and down to my core. "Come for us, Mädchen," he said. He sounded bored, but when I looked over at him, his eyes were riveted to the sight of my rolling hips and heaving breasts, his cheeks flushed and lips parted.

I came so hard it startled a shriek from me. Krampus kept nipping my breast and slammed my hips down against him so his cock ground almost painfully against my clit. His claws dug into my ass, little pinpricks of pain to contrast with the pleasure. Stars lit up my vision as the little death swept over me, blotting out every thought.

When the orgasm had passed, I slumped boneless against Krampus, panting hard. The ability to think slowly returned to me. Beneath me, my supernatural lover chuckled and his chest vibrated against mine. He patted my hair approvingly.

Nicholas lifted me from Krampus and carried me to the bathroom, where he ran me a bath. Then he climbed into the bathtub and I lowered myself down into his arms, settling against his chest. He used a loofah to scrub me gently, letting me rest boneless between his legs. His dick pressed against my rear, too worn out to achieve another erection any time soon.

Sometimes it felt like Nicholas enjoyed aftercare as much as sex. I was okay with that—grateful for it, even, especially when Krampus had no interest in it. Being loved by the Christmas devil was like being loved by a feral cat. Without Nicholas, I probably would have left him months ago, and without Krampus, something would have been missing. The two balanced each perfectly.

And, as Nicholas often reminded me, I was the missing piece of the puzzle to their happiness. Three was, as it turned out, the magic number.

After our bath, we dressed and went downstairs to find Krampus cooking dinner. From the smell, he was making pot roast and mashed potatoes, Nicholas's favorite. Krampus wasn't a demonstrative lover—he never said those three little words—but we knew he loved us because he cared for us like this. Intimacy terrified him, so I let him pretend to keep me at arm's length. Meanwhile, I knew he'd revert to a feral monster without me and Nicholas. Krampus knew it, too, and it petrified him, but we didn't make him talk about it. He was happiest not facing his feelings head-on, and we were okay with that. Maybe someday he'd learn to trust and open up, and we had all the time in the world to wait.

An elf the size of a 6-year-old scurried around on the counter top. She was Krampus's favorite of Nicholas's creations—not that Krampus would ever admit it. He'd nicknamed her Patty because her favorite candies were those delicious chocolate-covered peppermint patties. The elf was so cute it was almost unbearable, with huge eyes in a dainty, child-like face. She'd put her hair in pigtails that showed off her delicately pointed ears. Her hands were small and nimble, as Nicholas had made them, so the elves could help him build toys in the workshop.

Patty was pale and androgynous like the rest of the elves. The only substance Nicholas had to work with to create his helpers was snow, so they glowed bright white and sparkled in sunlight like Twilight vampires. At first they were relatively featureless, but with time and input from me and Krampus and the helpers themselves, Nicholas improved upon his original design until they looked almost human. In the last few months they'd started to choose names and even genders, and recently a few had requested some sculpting between their legs instead of smooth Barbie crotches.

Nicholas was hesitant because he didn't want horny elves running around the North Pole fucking on the tables where they made the toys. "This is a workshop, not a bordello," he'd said many times. My opinion on it was that he'd made living, conscious creatures who deserved to enjoy their lives, and if they wanted to have sex, wasn't that their right? They couldn't just make toys all day and call that a satisfying life.

He did the best he could with his little wards, but he was in way over his head. Another thing he liked to say was, "I'm a toy maker, not a father," whenever I brought up that he had created his helpers and now he was responsible for them. In the end he always did what the elves asked, and I knew it was only a matter of time before he gave in and let them have genitalia. He was too kind to do otherwise.

I wondered, though, if they'd be able to reproduce if Nicholas made them reproductive organs. What was the limit on Christmas magic? We hadn't found it yet, except the restrictions on leaving the North Pole outside of one night a year. And how adorable would tiny elf babies be? Probably ridiculously adorable. They'd be the size of hamsters.

"Hi Patty," I greeted the elf.

"You're going to say hi to me like you weren't just screaming so loud the whole village could hear you twenty minutes ago?" Patty asked, sliding carrot peels into a trash bag.

A flush crept up my neck. This was the only downside to having elves—they were around to hear what we got up to. And we got up to it a lot, which is probably why the elves wanted to try it.

I couldn't blame them. We did make it sound like a lot of fun. In a year, we hadn't lost interest in each other, either. The three of us were always finding new and exciting ways to enjoy each other.

"No need to be jealous," I quipped back at her. "Someday you'll get to scream like that, if you're very good."

Nicholas snorted. "Don't make promises you aren't going to have to keep."

Patty hopped from the counter to the center island where Nicholas and I sat on bar stools. She glared at Nicholas with her arms crossed over her little chest. "It's almost Christmas, and I thought you had to grant Christmas wishes."

Nicholas sighed. "Is the pot roast done yet?"

"Don't ignore me. I'm not letting this go!" Patty stomped her foot on the counter.

Nicholas glared at me. "Look what you've done."

I barked a laugh. "Look what *you've* done."

"You told me to recruit some help!"

"Yes, *recruit*, not create."

Krampus's tail lashed against the kitchen floor in irritation right before he grabbed Patty by the waist and moved her to the ground. "Get out of here. And you two," he turned to us, one clawed finger pointing at us each in turn, "stop arguing about this. You're ruining dinner. You know she's right, and you know he'll give in eventually. Just give him time." He turned back to the pot roast.

"I'm not letting this go!" Patty repeated as she made for the door.

Nicholas shouted something at her in the old Germanic language he and Krampus and the elves all speak. Something about remembering, probably remembering why she was created in the first place. Nicholas and Krampus had been teaching me the language but I wasn't quite fluent yet.

"See you for the stitch 'n bitch later, Noelle," Patty called down the hallway. I'd been teaching the elves how to knit, among other things. With their dexterous fingers, they excelled at it.

"Surely you can understand why she wants a vagina," I said as Krampus doled out slices of pot roast and portions of vegetables and mashed potatoes onto three plates. The elves never joined us for meals because their diets consisted entirely of candy. They didn't even want to be in the room if we were eating meat or vegetables. That served me just fine because it meant I got alone time with my guys.

"Of course I do," Nicholas said. "But vaginas cause trouble." He reached over and cupped me between the legs with one big hand.

Desire surged through me, like it always did at his touch.

"Eat," Krampus ordered, putting plates in front of both of us before serving his own. "I want you hale and hearty for round two." He winked at me.

My panties dampened between my legs. I'd been living at the North Pole for almost a year, but I was still mad for these men. Just a look from Krampus with those yellow eyes turned me into a puddle of lust.

I loved the quiet moments even more than the sex, though. The moments where Nicholas would read aloud from a book by the fire while I knit tiny mittens for the elves. Or when Krampus taught me how to bake babka, a Polish sweet bread. Or when we went for sleigh rides just to look at the stars, snuggled up under blankets and drinking hot chocolate from a thermos.

"It's almost your birthday," Nicholas observed as he cut into his meat.

Krampus grinned, biting into a chunk of carrot with his big, sharp fangs. His tail stroked my leg like he couldn't keep himself from touching me. "What's your Christmas wish this year, Mädchen?"

I looked from Nicholas to Krampus and back again. I couldn't suppress the smile that came to my lips. "I don't have one," I confessed.

"None?" Nicholas asked, cocking one eyebrow.

"None," I confirmed, beaming at both men. "I have every-thing I could ever want right here."

Nicholas grinned and Krampus flicked his tongue across his lips.

"Good girl."

About the Author

Sarah Hans loves writing about monsters. She used to be an administrative assistant, then a special education teacher, and now she's a full-time writer. Her books are primarily in the horror and dark fantasy romance genres, but she also writes science fiction and fantasy, and even a children's picture book. She believes that Black lives matter, trans rights are human rights, and it's nobody else's business what you do with your own body. She lives in Ohio with her amazing husband and an entirely reasonable number of teenagers and pets.

You can connect with me on:

- https://sarahhans.com
- https://www.facebook.com/SarahHansAuthor
- https://www.instagram.com/sarahhansauthor
- https://bsky.app/profile/sarahhans.bsky.social

Subscribe to my newsletter:

- http://bit.ly/4pvIIdo

Also by Sarah K. Hans

Other dark romances you should check out:

Rebel Omega

A post-apocalyptic Why Choose Omegaverse romance in a world where all Alphas are shifters and omegas are rare and precious.

King of Darkness

A standalone romantasy starring a naive princess and a demon shadow daddy! Inspired by the classic 1986 movie Legend, starring Tim Curry.

Insatiable

The first book in the Monster Escort Agency series! This is the story of Michelle, a lady of the night and tattoo artist who is wooed by four hot vampires. Very spicy!

www.ingramcontent.com/pod-product-compliance
Lightning Source LLC
Chambersburg PA
CBHW071133100726
47908CB00008B/2593